Hairy Maclary
from Donaldson's Dairy

Lynley Dodd

PUFFIN

Out of the gate
and off for a walk
went Hairy Maclary
from Donaldson's Dairy

and Hercules Morse
as big as a horse

with Hairy Maclary
from Donaldson's Dairy.

Bottomley Potts
covered in spots,
Hercules Morse
as big as a horse

and Hairy Maclary
from Donaldson's Dairy.

Muffin McLay
like a bundle of hay,
Bottomley Potts
covered in spots,
Hercules Morse
as big as a horse

and Hairy Maclary
from Donaldson's Dairy.

Bitzer Maloney
all skinny and bony,
Muffin McLay
like a bundle of hay,
Bottomley Potts
covered in spots,
Hercules Morse
as big as a horse

and Hairy Maclary
from Donaldson's Dairy.

Schnitzel von Krumm
with a very low tum,
Bitzer Maloney
all skinny and bony,
Muffin McLay
like a bundle of hay,
Bottomley Potts
covered in spots,
Hercules Morse
as big as a horse

and Hairy Maclary
from Donaldson's Dairy.

With tails in the air
they trotted on down
past the shops and the park
to the far end of town.
They sniffed at the smells
and they snooped at each door,
when suddenly,
out of the shadows
they
saw . . .

SCARFACE CLAW
the toughest Tom
in
town.

"EEEEEOWWWFFTZ!"
said Scarface Claw.

Off with a yowl
a wail and a howl,
a scatter of paws
and a clatter of claws,
went Schnitzel von Krumm
with a very low tum,
Bitzer Maloney
all skinny and bony,
Muffin McLay
like a bundle of hay,
Bottomley Potts
covered in spots,
Hercules Morse
as big as a horse

and Hairy Maclary
from Donaldson's Dairy,

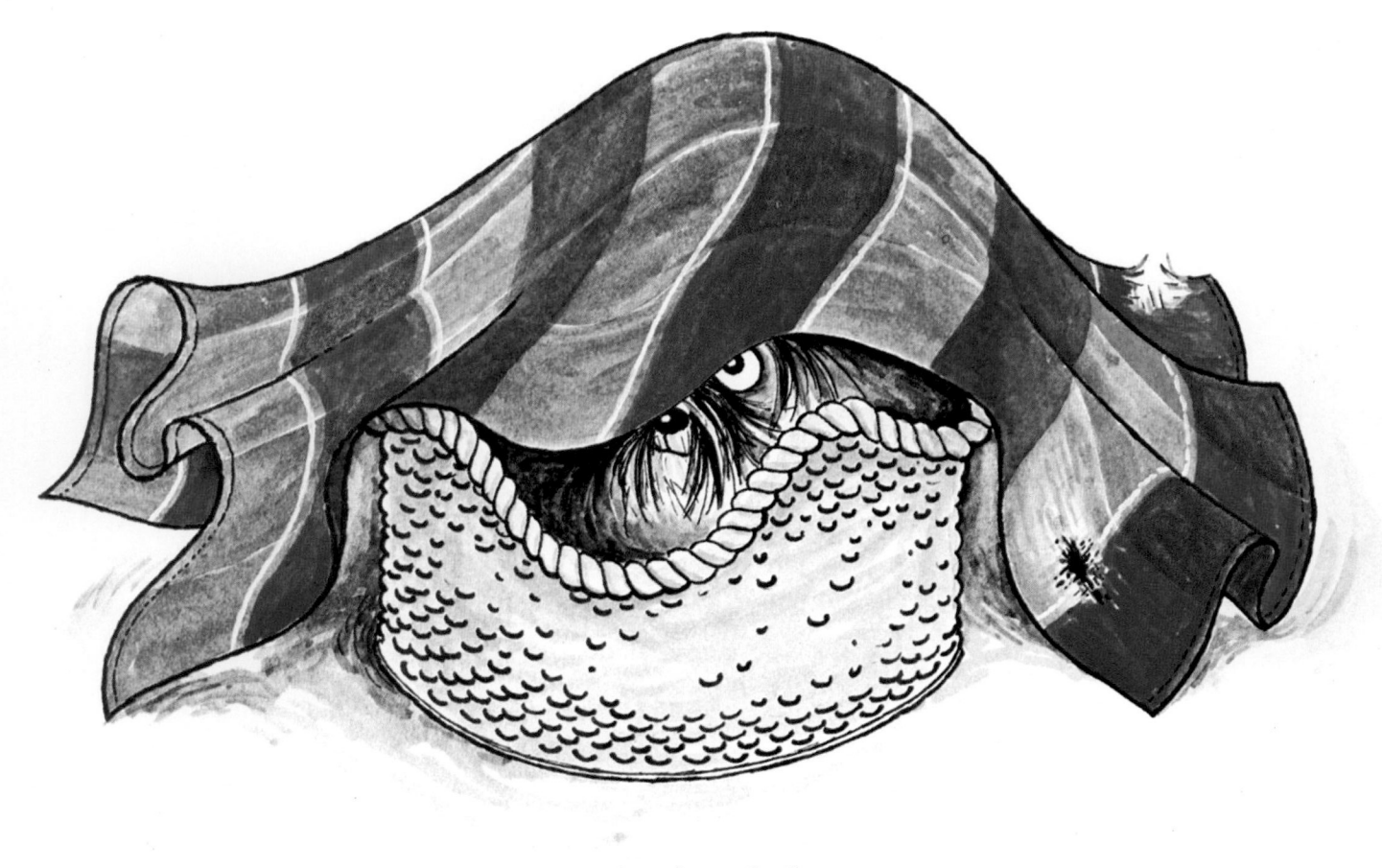

straight back home
to bed.

Hairy Maclary's Bone

Lynley Dodd

PUFFIN

Down in the town
by the butcher's shop door,
sat Hairy Maclary
from Donaldson's Dairy.

Out of the door
came Samuel Stone.
He gave Hairy Maclary
his tastiest
bone.

Then off up the street
on scurrying feet,
on his way to the dairy
went Hairy Maclary.

And chasing him home,
with their eyes on the bone,
went Hercules Morse,
Bottomley Potts,
Muffin McLay,
Bitzer Maloney
and Schnitzel von Krumm
with the very low tum.

Hungrily sniffing
and licking their chops,
they followed him up
past the school and the shops.

They came to the sign
selling Sutherland's Sauce.
Through they all went —

except Hercules Morse.

They came to a hedge
along Waterloo Way.
Under they went —

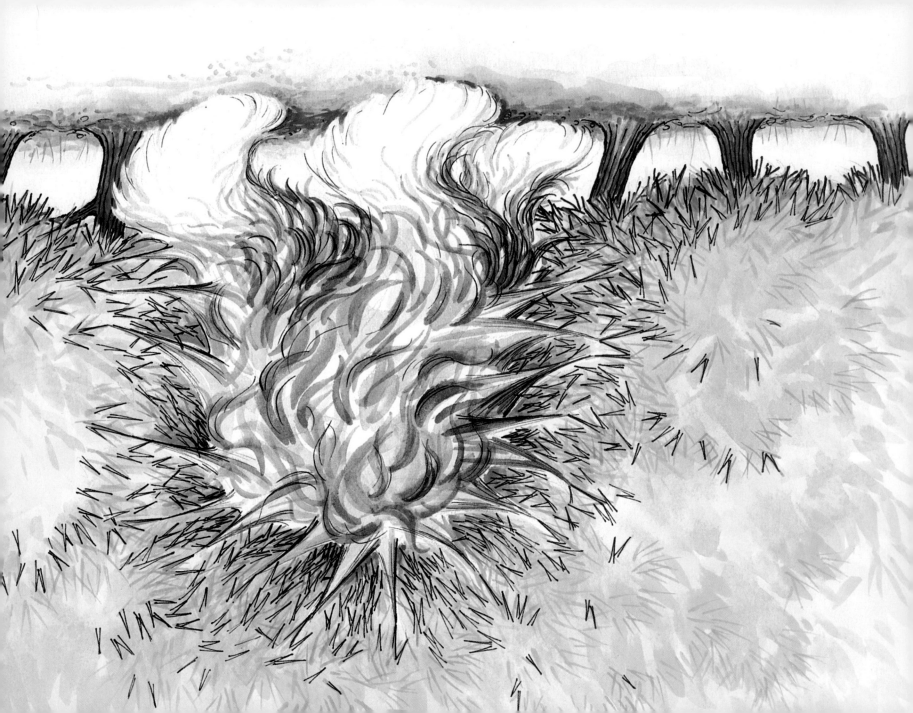

except Muffin McLay.

They came to a yard
full of dinghies and yachts.
Round they all went —

except Bottomley Potts.

They came to a building site,
cluttered and stony.
Over they went —

except Bitzer Maloney.

They came to a wall
by the house of Miss Plum.
One of them jumped —

but not Schnitzel von Krumm.

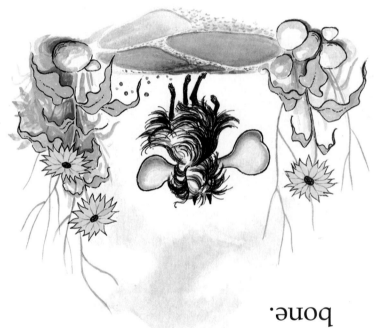

So at last he was free
to go home on his own,
Hairy Maclary
with ALL of his
bone.

Hairy Maclary, SIT

Lynley Dodd

PUFFIN

Something was happening
down in the Park;
such a yap
could be heard,
such a blusterous bark.
A fidget of dogs
lined up on the grass
for the Kennel Club's
Special
Obedience
Class.

Hairy Maclary
felt breezily bad,
jittery, skittery,
mischievous,
mad.
The leader said
'SIT!'
but he wouldn't obey.
The other dogs sat
but he scampered
away.

Galloping here,
galloping there,
rollicking,
frolicking,
EVERYWHERE.

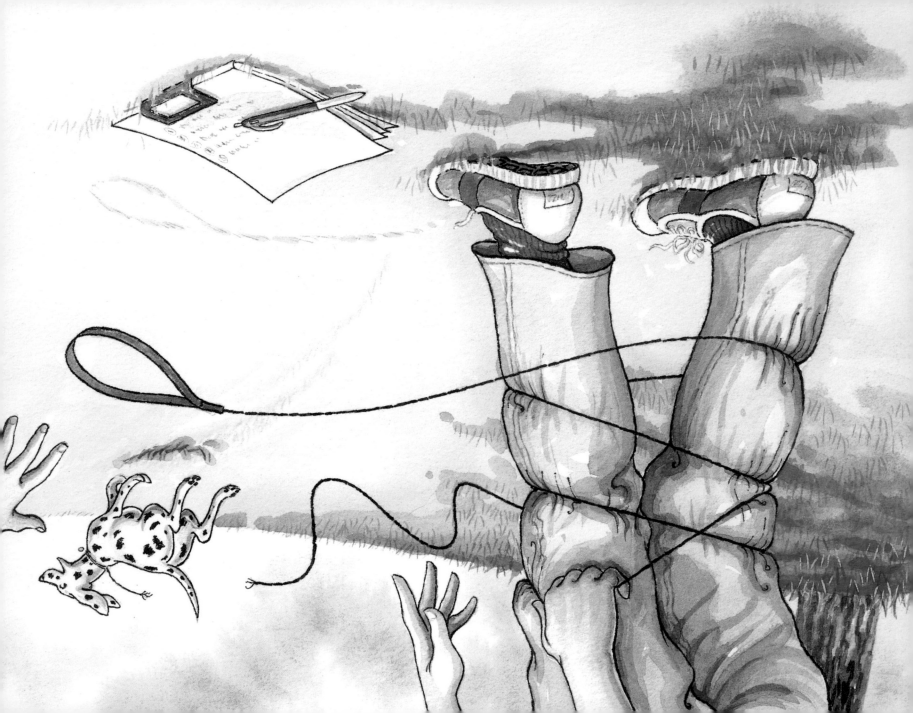

'DOWN!'
called the leader,
so tangled in knots
that
off in a hurry
sped Bottomley Potts.

Galloping here,
galloping there,
rollicking,
frolicking,
EVERYWHERE.

'HEEL!'
cried the leader
but
skipping away
to follow the others
went Muffin McLay.

Galloping here,
galloping there,
rollicking,
frolicking,
EVERYWHERE.

'STAY!'
roared the leader,
husky and hoarse,
but
out of his clutches
slipped Hercules Morse.

Galloping here,
galloping there,
rollicking,
frolicking,
EVERYWHERE.

'COME!'
howled the leader
but
looking for fun
were Bitzer Maloney
and Schnitzel von Krumm.

Galloping here,
galloping there,
rollicking,
frolicking,
EVERYWHERE.

'WAIT!'
yelled the leader
but
capering free
went Custard
and Noodle
and Barnacle B.

Galloping here,
galloping there,
rollicking,
frolicking,
EVERYWHERE.

They raced round the fountain,
they chased through the trees,
they barged over gardens
and scattered the leaves.
They hurtled past sheds
and the bandstand beyond;
they rushed through a hedge
and
went ...

SPLAT
in the
pond.

PUFFIN BOOKS

Published by the Penguin Group: London, New York, Australia,
Canada, India, Ireland, New Zealand and South Africa
Penguin Books Ltd, Registered Offices: 80 Strand, London WC2R 0RL, England

puffinbooks.com

Hairy Maclary from Donaldson's Dairy
First published in New Zealand by Mallinson Rendell Publishers Ltd 1983
Published in Picture Puffins 1985
Hairy Maclary's Bone
First published in New Zealand by Mallinson Rendell Publishers Ltd 1984
Published in Picture Puffins 1986
Hairy Maclary, Sit
First published in New Zealand by Mallinson Rendell Publishers Ltd 1997
Published in Picture Puffins 1999
This edition first published in Puffin Books 2011

001 – 10 9 8 7 6 5 4 3 2 1

Made and printed in China
ISBN: 978-0-141-34267-2